DISCARD

FRANKLY
SCARLETT,
I DO GIVE A
DAMN!

FRANKLY
SCARLETT,
I DO GIVE A
DAMN!

Classic Romances Retold

BEVERLY WEST
and NANCY K. PESKE

HarperCollins*Publishers*

HarperCollins books may be purchased for educational, business, or sales promotional use. For information please write: Special Markets Department, HarperCollins Publishers, Inc., 10 East 53rd Street, New York, NY 10022.

FIRST EDITION

Designed by Nancy Singer

Library of Congress Cataloging-in-Publication Data

West, Beverly, 1961–
Frankly Scarlett, I do give a damn! : classic romances retold / by Beverly West and Nancy K. Peske. — 1st ed.
          p.   cm.
          ISBN 0-06-017389-0
1. Love stories—Adaptations.   2. Humorous stories.   3. Political correctness—Humor.   I. Peske, Nancy K., 1962–   .   II. Title.
          PN6162.W453   1995
813'.54—dc20   95-42486

96 97 98 99 00 ❖ / HC 10 9 8 7 6 5 4 3 2 1

To our grandmother LaVerne Anderson Peske, who taught us how to play poker and how to shoot the moon, and to our moms, Marilyn Knox and Sally Powell, who taught us to go for the happy ending

Acknowledgments

Thanks to our agent, Kevin "Our Hero" McShane.

Thanks also to all our friends at HarperCollins, especially Susan Weinberg, Sherri Weiss, and most especially our editor, Mauro DiPreta.

And as always, thanks to George "I enjoy vacuuming" Darrow.

Contents

∞

Contents

∞

Introduction

As modern women we reject the lessons we have learned from the great romances of literature, which always seem to end tragically, at least for the woman. We asked ourselves, how could these star-crossed disasters have been averted? Surely there must be some way for love to flourish without some poor unfortunate heroine throwing herself on the train tracks or giving in to consumption.

Frankly, we think that if our romantic heroes had learned to behave like responsible adults, and perhaps done a little more relationship work, events wouldn't have turned out so badly. If only Adam had supported Eve's roving intellectual curiosity and encouraged her to fulfill herself outside of the home, perhaps there would still be paradise on earth.

And what if Heathcliff had realized that storming angrily onto the moors was not a healthy way of dealing with anger?

Or if Jane Eyre's beloved Mr. Rochester had conquered his fear and confronted difficult emotional issues instead of locking them away in his attic, along with his first wife? Or if just once in the course of great literary romance, the man had turned to the woman and said, "Darling, I'm sorry, I was wrong, and you, as usual, are absolutely right in everything that you have said to me. I will do better in the future and am deeply grateful that you have found some way, in your understanding, tender, and nurturing heart (and by that I don't mean to imply that you are relegated strictly to maternal stereotypes) to forgive me. Oh, by the way, I took out the garbage."

With these thoughts in mind, we have reconstructed twelve romances to explore the possibilities of improved gender relations within the timeless love stories of great literature. We think you will agree that if only Rhett Butler or Jay Gatsby had read *The Dance of Anger* or attended a John Gray seminar they would have saved our favorite heroines a world of grief.

I

Gone With the Wind

(Or, Frankly Scarlett, I Do Give a Damn!)

Scarlett O'Hara was not beautiful but men seldom realized it when caught by her charms, her keen intellect, her independent spirit, and her considerable depth of character, all of which men valued far more than a pretty face or a seventeen-inch waist. Scarlett could have had her pick of any of the young bucks in the county. Unfortunately, as a result of self-esteem issues, she set her sights on the tall, handsome, golden-haired Ashley Wilkes, whose reserved demeanor was not really an indication of masculine strength but rather of a deep-seated fear of intimacy.

Ashley's boundary issues and his reluctance to embrace

change led him to marry his cousin Melanie. In a typical male projection, Ashley believed that his fiancée was a mere reflection of himself, not recognizing that she was a pillar of soft-spoken feminine power who represented the enduring spirit of the conquered South—minus its racism, classism, and wholesale destruction and exploitation of innocent plant crops.

"She's just like me, Scarlett, part of my blood, and we understand each other," Ashley explained, attempting to rationalize his inability to bond with a woman who had a well-developed sense of self.

Scarlett, not one for avoidance behavior, replied, "Why don't you say it, you coward? You're afraid to marry me!" and punctuated her message nonverbally with a sobering slap to Ashley's cheek. Unfortunately, this did not jar loose Ashley's innermost emotions, so mired was he in his masculist dysfunction.

Happily for Scarlett, this exchange was overheard by a rakish yet sensitive and supportive visitor from Charleston, Captain Rhett Butler. Rhett, despite the many years of immersion in a warring male culture dedicated to brutality and oppression, instantly recognized Scarlett for the fully realized, actuated, multifaceted woman that she was.

"You, my dear Ms. O'Hara, are a girl—excuse me, a woman—of rare spirit, and Mr. Wilkes should thank God on bended knee—without putting you on a sexist pedestal—for a woman with your passion for living," said Rhett, clearly demonstrating that he was a man worthy of Scarlett's indomitable inner strength because he shared her ability to confront difficult emotions and work through conflicts in a healthy manner.

The brokenhearted Scarlett did not immediately recognize her soulmate, sad to say. She was distracted by a couple of bad marriages, the fall of the South, the death of both of her parents, her only child, and her beloved Melanie, with whom she had bonded in their mutual struggle against patriarchy and the Yankees, and the near loss of her familial home, whose verdant acres meant more to her than life itself. Twelve years later, Scarlett realized that Rhett was her own true love and her life partner of choice, not because she needed a man to be a whole person, but because she saw the possibility for a mutually satisfying and fulfilling partnership between equals.

Allowing herself to be vulnerable, Scarlett confessed this epiphany to Rhett.

"Rhett, tonight when I knew, I ran home every step of the way to tell you I—"

Rhett, sensing her emotional discomfort without her having to express it, stepped in, willing to share the burden of this difficult confrontation.

"Scarlett, I realize that the confines of the antebellum South's restricted vision of womanhood has been a tremendous obstacle in your path toward self-realization. Although it has taken you twelve years to appreciate me and how much I love you and value you as an individual, I'm here for you."

"You mean you still love me after all of this?" Scarlett exclaimed, incredulous at the depth of his understanding, sensitivity, constancy, insightfulness, caring, gentleness, and masculine strength.

"Frankly Scarlett, I *do* give a damn," said Rhett. Scarlett collapsed into his arms, not because she was physically inferior, but because she had learned to surrender her illusion of control in the interests of establishing trust and intimacy with her life partner of choice.

After reaffirming their commitment to a loving, symbiotic, monogamous relationship, Scarlett and Rhett resolved to work on improving their communication skills in order to avoid future misunderstandings. They vowed to put the past behind them and start a new life.

"But where shall we go, what shall we do?" asked Scarlett, who had ideas of her own but was committed to more open lines of communication and a sharing of the burden of common decision making.

"Let's go to your place," said Rhett, knowing that Tara was

a touchstone for her. "I'll cook you a nice dinner, I'll lay a fire, and, with your consent, we can make passionate love, during which I will be as concerned with your pleasure as my own. Then while you nap, I will wash the dishes and prepare a light, healthy snack to restore our expended energy."

As they hugged in the light of the setting sun, the wind tousling their hair, Rhett added, "Just don't let the uncertainty of our future as citizens of a post-Reconstruction Southern society muddy your enjoyment of the moment. After all, tomorrow is another day."

2

Wuthering Heights

(Or, Alternative Arrangements for the Weekend)

ome children, see what I have brought you," said Mister Earnshaw, the old master who, despite this elitist eighteenth-century courtesy title, was actually a firm but gentle single parent, struggling with the demands of responsible child rearing. "I've carried it all the way from Liverpool."

Peering out of the bundle that Mr. Earnshaw held in his arms was a dirty, ragged, dark-haired Gypsy child born without the advantages of a high socioeconomic status or even a last name. Ms. Cathy, though hardly six years old, had nevertheless rejected the class distinctions and racial prejudice of the day and immediately adopted this urchin of color, Heathcliff, as her closest confidant.

As the years passed and Ms. Cathy came of age, she developed a budding attraction to Heathcliff, who was darkly handsome, in touch with his sensuality, connected to the animal within, and looked damn fine in a pair of leather riding breeches. For his part, Heathcliff wanted nothing more than to gather heather from the moors for his beloved Cathy, support her efforts to defy the oppressive conventions of late-eighteenth-century England, and help develop her capacity for multiple orgasms.

What should have been a naturally unfolding, free exchange between equals dedicated to plumbing the depths of their sensual natures was thwarted by a misunderstanding borne of the rigid social mores of the time, which did not value strong-headed heroines with a capacity for multiple orgasms.

Ms. Cathy, unable to defy social convention as a consequence of a separation anxiety created by the early death of her mother, considered marrying the boy next door, Edgar Linton. Linton provided social position and security but was rather quick on the trigger and didn't even own a pair of leather breeches, much less a riding crop.

"Oh, Nelly, what shall I do?" bemoaned Cathy, confiding

her innermost fears to her beloved surrogate mother figure. "Truly I should marry Linton, for he is handsome and well born and rich, and he loves me, and certainly, to marry Heathcliff would degrade me in the eyes of proper society, but it is Heathcliff with whom I belong. It is Heathcliff I love. It is Heathcliff who knows where my G spot is."

Unbeknownst to the troubled Catherine, the impetuous Heathcliff had overheard the beginning of her speech. He jumped to conclusions before hearing the whole story, which was to be expected given his own insecurities arising from his deprived early childhood and troubled adolescence. Heathcliff rushed out onto the windswept moors, bellowing his inner angst to the indifferent heavens, before heading off to make a killing in real estate. Poor Heathcliff foolishly believed that the way to Cathy's heart was through her pocketbook rather than through her erogenous zones.

Not knowing where her beloved Heathcliff had gone, Cathy unfortunately settled for the inferior Linton, who provided a stable home life but left her sexually unfulfilled. Years later, when Heathcliff returned, financially solvent, his manhood straining against his fine tailored trousers, Ms. Cathy was forced to acknowledge that financial stability and social position were a sorry substitute for foreplay.

Forlorn and frustrated, Cathy took to her bed for some

much needed centering and some time out to reacquaint herself with her sexual response.

Suddenly, she heard a knock at the door.

"What do you want?" Cathy called out crossly, having just managed to awaken the first stirrings of forgotten passion.

A timid Linton responded, "Darling, Heathcliff and I have just shared a glass of chilled chardonnay and would like to share our thoughts with you. We're concerned about your physical, emotional, and sexual health and think we've come up with a viable solution."

"Couldn't it wait five minutes?" asked Cathy, who had learned to assert herself even in the face of testosterone-motivated male rivalry that completely objectified women.

The two men, having no intention to rob her of her personhood and certainly wishing to validate her ability to communicate her needs in an open and honest manner, waited patiently before knocking again.

"What now?" Cathy asked with a clouded brow, skeptical about the ability of men to truly understand a woman's needs and vexed that they had polished off her last good bottle of chardonnay.

"You and Edgar have broken my heart, Heathcliff, and you both come to bewail the deed to me, as if you were the people to be pitied. I shall not pity you, not I. And why have you finished my last bottle of good chardonnay?" Her present countenance had a wild vindictiveness in her white cheek, and a bloodless lip, and a scintillating eye.

"Forgive me my beloved," said Heathcliff, "but I could no longer bear the torment of your suffering, or Linton's beer. Haunt me, be with me always, take any form, drive me mad, only don't leave me alone in this abyss where I cannot find you and must resort to fermented hops."

"Listen, darling," Linton interrupted politely, "I've obviously been unable to satisfy you, probably because I am a hypercivilized aristocrat disconnected from my animalistic male essence, and I'm British. But Heath and I have agreed that there is no reason for you to have to choose between social acceptability and multiple orgasms. A woman of your obvious complexity, who is able to straddle both her intellectual and sexual selves, should be able to experience all that life has to offer. Therefore, we've decided to establish an alternative marital arrangement, whereby you can pursue your activities as a prominent social matron during the week with me and plumb the depths of your sexual nature with Heathcliff on the weekends. Would that be acceptable to you?"

"That's very supportive of you, Edgar," Ms. Cathy smiled, "and the plan sounds fine with me, except for one small change. Although today is a weekday, would you mind leaving Heathcliff and I alone for a few moments? We'll join you later to watch the sun sink over the moors behind my beloved Wuthering Heights."

"I'm so happy we were able to discuss this openly and I wouldn't dream of interrupting your long-awaited reunion with the man who so obviously ignites your passionate nature. I'll just trot on down to the cellar and chill a couple bottles of buttery white burgundy."

Local legend has it that when the moon is full and the heather has just begun to bloom, you can still see this happy threesome wandering the windswept moors.

3

The Iliad

(Or, Helen of Troy, the Female Separatist Alternative Grunge Years)

ing, O Goddess, of the lust of Paris, son of Priam, who brought countless ills upon his countrymen because he couldn't keep his pants zipped, and of the anger of Menelaus, who brought grief to the Achaeans. Having lost the affections of the marvelously and divinely lovely, self-actualized, and non-codependent Helen, Paris led the Achaeans into war. All of this could, of course, have been averted if only he'd learned to be a little more sensitive to the needs of this titled, beautiful, sensual, independent, and intelligent woman living within the confines of an ancient patriarchal culture and ironed his own damn togas. I mean, okay, so he was a king, but he was an old fart, and he demanded extra starch.

And so it came to pass that when Paris, son of Priam, Prince of Troy, who not only had comely locks and a bag of love tricks but played a mean lead lyre in an alternative Trojan band, landed on Achaean shores, Helen resolved to go with him back to Troy and sing backing vocals. Menelaus, upon hearing of her plans, cried out to Olympus, and Zeus, who also liked his togas pressed with extra starch and could therefore empathize with the loss of a good laundress, heeded his lament. Zeus called forth to Menelaus' proud and fierce brother, Agamemnon, to rouse Achilles, Herakles, and all the Achaeans, and as when some mighty wave that thunders on the beach when the west wind has lashed it into fury, even so did the serried phalanxes of the Danians march steadfastly to battle.

"Excuse me, but what gave you the idea that you could just march a bunch of serried phalanxes in here without checking with me first?" demanded Helen, who had a very healthy sense of boundaries. "This is so typical. You never ask me my opinion about anything. It's always 'Pour me a liba-tion, Helen,' 'Slaughter a fatted calf for dinner, Helen,' 'Go launch a thousand ships, Helen.' I'm sick of it, I tell you, sick of it. I'm leaving you and running off with Paris. *He* is a man of fair favor. *He* has gifts that golden Venus has given him. *He* doesn't need to prove his manhood by starting a world war, and *he* sends his laundry out."

At that point, Paris stepped out of Helen's chamber, his comely locks flashing golden in the afterglow. He stamped out his Lucky Strike on the floor and spake thus to Menelaus:

"I could crush you like a filterless cigarette against the stones of my passion, you old Attic fart. Look at you, with your spindly legs and your hoary pate. All the Danian phalanxes in the world can't resurrect your shriveled manhood. If you don't watch it, I'm going to smote you but good."

"Yeah, you and what army?" Menelaus snorted. He raised his mighty sword, preparing to run Paris through. "And lest you forget, I have Zeus on my side."

"Yeah, well Minerva favors me."

"Yeah, well Athena thinks I'm comely."

"Yeah, well Venus smiles upon the Trojans."

"Oh, who cares what that old whore thinks about—"

"What a bunch of linear masculist creeps!" said Helen. "I hope you realize that this kind of behavior will lay the foundations for a tyrannical patriarchal religion that imposes its own limited moral structure upon the less fortunate of the world through economic and spiritual exploitation of the masses. Take your pantheon and shove it, both of you, I'm not going anywhere with either one of you."

"But sweet pea," protested Paris, "if you don't come with me, there'll be no Trojan War, there'll be no glorious epic poems celebrating the senseless slaughter of thousands, no linear narrative structure, no oral tradition, no Western canon. People will trust Greeks bearing gifts and drugstores will only stock Sheik, Fiesta, and Gold Coin. We will lose the entire foundation of Western civilization."

"And good riddance, too," said Helen, who straightened her shoulders, threw her head back, and declared, "I've had enough of this—none of you ever flipped my switch in the bedchamber anyway. Ever since I got back from that retreat during last spring's Dionysian Festival where I communed with nature, running through the hillsides rending the flesh of wild animals, singing melodies in the Phrygian mode, and cavorting with satyrs, I just haven't felt fulfilled. And now, when the moon is full and the grapes are heavy on the vines, I can feel my blood raging, hot and primal, and I long to tear apart any man I come across and devour his flesh."

Menelaus, Paris, Agamemnon, Achilles, Herakles, and all of the serried phalanxes of Danians grew deadly silent and clutched their collective girdle.

Helen, empowered by the feminine force within her, continued, eyes shining with a strange hunger. "There's a little island called Lesbos, where womyn like me, who are unhappy being crushed by the sandal of the patriarchy, embrace communal living and goddess worship. They are sufficient unto themselves and spend their days singing love dithyrambs to the strains of a discordant lyre and developing their own herstory. Their lead singer, Sappho, could probably use a passionate, confident, and committed ululator. I am resolved to go to Lesbos, to develop my ululating skills, to take up the bass lyre, to never again shave under my arms or allow myself to become the property of any man or masculist state. Have your war if you must, but this face ain't launching diddly, and I'm not cleaning up the empty libation goblets the day after either."

Thus spake Helen, who turned on her heel and went off to found her own herstory and influence generations of alternative female grungers, Riot Grrrrrls, and Bitches With Attitude.

4

Adam and Eve

(Or, Trouble in Paradise)

n the beginning, God created the heavens and the earth. And God said, Let there be light, and there was light. God saw that the light was good. And God said, Let the water under the sky be gathered to one place, and let the dry ground appear. God saw that the land was good. And God said, Let the land produce vegetation and living creatures according to their kind. And God saw that the plants and the animals were good. Then God said, Let us produce man in our image, only with better hair and more upper body development. And God saw that Adam was good. Then God said, Let us create a helpmate for Adam. We will make woman from

Adam's rib, also in our likeness only with long legs, a few more curves, and a tempting décolletage. And God saw that Eve was definitely going to cause some problems.

"Listen, Adam," God said, "I've given you a helpmate to assist you in the garden, but she's a really hot number and you are going to have your hands full. You turn your back, next thing you know, she'll be talking to crafty serpents and eating forbidden fruit. So be fruitful and multiply, keep her barefoot and pregnant, but whatever you do, don't let her into the middle of the garden alone to dally with reptiles beneath the Tree of the Knowledge of Good and Evil."

And so Adam kept close watch over his wife. He was constantly by her side and didn't allow her to work outside the garden or take consciousness-raising classes. One day, while Adam was off exercising dominion over the animals, Eve heard a deep and sultry voice calling her into the middle of the garden, where she encountered a serpent.

"Hey baby," hissed the serpent. "What's a hot-looking helpmate like you doing with a working stiff like Adam anyway? Okay, so he has dominion over the fish of the sea and the birds of the air and the beasts of the field, but I'm an international investor with a well-diversified portfolio and an MBA. I can give you knowledge of good and evil, and the occasional weekend in Paris during fashion season. What do you say?

Why don't you come on over here and check out my apples?"

"God said I mustn't touch the apples on the Tree of the Knowledge of Good and Evil or I will surely die," said Eve, who was hopelessly mired in restrictive Judeo-Christian notions of appropriate female behavior.

"Don't you realize that the patriarchy is denying you knowledge of good and evil for the sole purpose of keeping you dependent upon their tyrannical power structure? They don't want you to eat the fruit of wisdom because information is power, and they fear that if you were properly educated, your superior female strength might one day rise up and challenge their compulsive male need to control the garden. I don't want to see that happen to you. I think you are a woman who is possessed of a powerful spirit and a keen intellect, in addition to a charming décolletage, and I want to see you maximize your full potential as the mother of the human race. So what do you say, just a little bite?"

Eve saw that the fruit of the tree was pleasing to the eye and also desirable for gaining wisdom, and would probably taste really great in a pie shell warm from the oven with a dollop of vanilla ice cream on top. So she took some and ate it, and just as she did so, Adam charged into the center of the garden.

"Eve, no! You must not eat from the fruit of the Tree of the Knowledge of Good and Evil or we shall surely die."

"Oh, come off it, Adam," said Eve, her mouth tingling with new sensual awareness. "I've had just about enough of you telling me what I can and cannot do around here—eat this, don't eat that, be fruitful, don't talk to serpents. It's enough to drive a girl mad! Things are going to change around here. First, I need a wardrobe. I can't go anywhere looking like this. I mean, I'm naked for heaven's sake! Second, things are going to have to be fifty-fifty between us. You're going to have to do the dishes every now and again, and I want free rein in the garden. Finally, you're just going to have to eat of the fruit of the tree of knowledge right along with me, because if you don't you're not going to be a suitable challenge to my roving and curious intellect. So what do you say? Those are my terms, take it or leave it."

And so Adam ate of the apple. Then the eyes of both of them were open and Adam realized that he too needed a wardrobe. They sewed fig leaves together and made coverings for themselves until such time as God might create the department store, providing the latest in designer fashions from around the world.

Then the man and his wife heard the sound of the Lord God as he was walking in the garden in the cool of the day and they hid from the Lord God among the trees of the garden.

"Adam, come out from behind that cyprus tree. Don't you

know you can't hide from the Lord your God? I'm omniscient, for heaven's sake."

Adam appeared, looking sheepish. "Um, sorry, God. We hid because we were ashamed of being naked."

"Why would you be ashamed? Did I not give you good upper body development and great hair? Did I not bless you with a helpmate possessed of a fetching décolletage? And who told you you were naked, anyway? Wait a minute, is that apple stuck between your teeth?"

"She made me do it," said Adam, pointing at Eve.

"I told you to watch her. I told you to keep her on a short leash, but you didn't listen, and now I am going to have to evict you. You know the rules of your lease. Eve, because you have done this, I will greatly increase your pains in childbearing. Cursed are you and all of your daughters. Because of you there will be witch trials, white slave trade, women will be unable to inherit property or attend law school until at least the twentieth century, and there will be no female abstract expressionists. I curse you with the desire to wear high heels and the need to wear restrictive undergarments to counteract the curse of gravity. I curse you with PMS—"

"Hold it," said Eve, glaring at the Lord her God. "What are you gonna curse him with?"

"I don't know. Male pattern balding?"

"That doesn't seem fair," said Adam, placing a loving arm around his wife's shoulders. "I mean, it could just as easily have been me. How 'bout I take the PMS and you give her the male pattern balding?"

"You mean you're willing to share equal responsibility and accept half the weight of my wrath?"

"Yes, because now that I have eaten of the fruit of the Tree of the Knowledge of Good and Evil, I realize that the rules of the garden are not conducive to growth, independence, creativity, or intimacy. If we are to contribute to the planet and be helpmates to one another, we must have free will, the power to exercise it according to our individual consciences, and durable, comfortable, yet flattering clothing that doesn't need dry cleaning, because these fig leaves are starting to itch."

God smiled upon his children.

"Adam, that's exactly the conclusion I had hoped that you would arrive at. To be a man, one must take responsibility for one's actions, listen to one's conscience, and treat one's helpmate like a respected and valued peer. The true measure of a man is not how much power he wields over the birds of the air and the beasts of the field but how honest he can be with himself and others. Here, wear these Birkenstocks and this preshrunk, unbleached natural-fiber clothing. Go forth now into the world and create art, music, literature, poetry, and always remember to recycle."

And so the first children of God went forth to establish an alternative to Western civilization that would value man's connectedness to the environment, where women could be strong and men tender, where there were no pesticides, no wars, no shopping malls, and no male pattern balding or PMS.

5

Casablanca

(Or, The Beginning of a Beautiful Relationship)

With the coming of the Second World War, many eyes turned from Europe toward America. Everybody was desperate for a ticket on the red-eye out of Lisbon to New York, and they didn't honor frequent flyer miles. A torturous roundabout refugee trail sprung up, Paris to Marseilles, across the Mediterranean to Moran, then by train or auto to some remote desert outpost called Casablanca, selected seemingly at random—or perhaps because Warner Brothers still had that Ali Baba set on the back lot. Here the fortunate ones might obtain exit visas, but the others wait in Casablanca, and wait, and wait, and wait.

Fortunately for those waiting, there was Rick's, a popular atmospheric airport bar with a Moroccan theme. Everybody went to Rick's because it had everything one needs: reasonably priced drinks, a smoking section, rousing singalongs, hypercaffeinated extras in fezzes, and fresh Goldfish crackers.

Rick's also had Rick, a proprietor with a resonant baritone, a quiet but commanding masculine presence, and an immaculate white tux that strained against his broad shoulders as he inhaled and exhaled exotic foreign tobacco, unaware of its devastating effect upon his cardiovascular system, as well as every woman in the room.

Unfortunately for those women, not only was Rick exposing them to the carcinogens in secondhand smoke, but he was also emotionally toxic. Out of touch with his feminine side and repressing his sentimentalist inner essence, when it came to relationships Rick was as noncommittal as unoccupied France, as remote as Casablanca itself, and as unavailable as decaf in an espresso bar.

This emotional aridity did not result from a disrespect for women but rather from the pain, the shame, and the blame that was Paris. This brief but obsessive love montage, poignantly scored by Academy Award–winning conductor Max Steiner and costarring an ethereally beautiful Swedish starlet who transcended the hollow, arctic stereotypes of Nordic beauties perpetuated by Hollywood, had left him psychologically scarred, emotionally unavailable, and patently unable to listen to "As Time Goes By" without resorting to negative drinking behaviors.

That fateful evening when Ilsa Lazlo entered stage left, Rick knew that nothing would ever be the same again. For one thing, Ilsa provided a pivotal plot point just when the intrigue was beginning to lose its momentum. For another thing, he was going to have to wrestle with his inner demons until he sprung for a jukebox that did not feature timeless and heartrending hits from yesteryear, destined to drive a man to drink.

Unable to resist watching him French-inhale one last time and frustrated by the bar's lack of a paging system, Ilsa made a fateful request, which she knew would bring Rick running.

"Play it for me, Sam," she said, her eyes brimming with ethereal Swedish tears of regret over having sacrificed a relationship with a man who made smoking look like a religious experience. "Play it once, Sam. For old time's sake. Play it, Sam. Play 'As Time Goes By.' Sing it, Sam. No, that's the harmony line, not the melody. Not so much vibrato. No, that's not the left-hand part . . ." Ilsa remembered Paris and, damn it, she wanted her reminiscence properly scored.

Horrified that Sam had not only played the forbidden song but blown the phrasing on the second verse, Rick rushed over. "Sam, I thought I told you never to play—" He stopped. "Ilsa."

"Rick. Won't you sit down and have a drink?"

"Oh no, Miss Ilsa," said Sam, "Mr. Rick never drinks with customers."

"Double tequila shooter with a beer chaser," Rick snapped at the waiter, unaware that he could indulge in a far healthier method of stress management such as Tai Chi, although it would be a little difficult to perform in the middle of a black-market Bloomingdale's without knocking over a few ficas and fezzes.

"I was just remembering Paris. You remember, Rick, don't you?"

"How could I forget? The Germans wore gray. You wore blue."

Rick had developed a penchant for using immortal one-liners as avoidance behavior.

"Actually," said Ilsa, "I think it was more of a teal, with a charming peplum and a capped sleeve and princess piping at the collar. And the Germans were in more of a dove gray."

"What are we going to do now?" Rick asked, looking deep into her eyes. "Who are you really and what were you before? What did you do and what did you think? And what the hell is teal?"

"Rick, we said no questions."

"Of all the cheap gin joints in all the towns in all the world, why did you have to walk into mine?"

"Oh, Rick, you wouldn't understand." Ilsa turned away, too distraught to explain the complex backstory involving resistance fighter Victor Lazlo and her characteristically feminine need to nurture and sustain her surrogate father figure, even at the expense of her own romantic yearnings, much less describe the distinction between blue and teal.

Just then, Lazlo returned from the bar with six tequila shooters and three Bud Lights and sat down next to Ilsa.

"Rick, let me introduce myself. I'm Victor Lazlo, Ilsa's husband, a martyr for the cause and a man more than willing to subjugate his own needs to the greater good. I can see very clearly that we are on our way to a bittersweet ending, where two young lovers must separate, sacrificing youthful passion in the cause of more mature but less ardent love. Take it from an old resistance fighter like me, self-sacrifice isn't all it's cracked up to be, and in fact, youthful passion is a very important milepost on the road to mature and lasting love. Now I realize my mere presence is throwing a cog into the wheel of a classic romance—"

"Oh dear," sighed Ilsa, flustered by the trio's dilemma and aware that if Rick took just one more drag off that cigarette she would be mere resin on his fingertips, "I can't think anymore. Rick, you do the thinking for both of us."

"That's a rather surprising sentiment, Ilsa, especially coming from an independent and courageous Swedish starlet who will one day break all the rules, trading a promising commercial career in America for an alternative lifestyle abroad."

Ilsa frowned. "I might be a strong, independent, and courageous woman who redefines feminine archetypes, but that doesn't mean that I don't have a postfeminist need for romance. All I'm asking is that you intuit my needs and make the correct decision for everyone involved. I don't think I'm expecting too much, here, do you?"

"Look," Lazlo interjected, "maybe I have a solution here. I have always dreamed of establishing a utopian community that does not place any boundaries on national, moral, or sexual preferences, a place that would be a heaven on earth, where every day is like a brief but obsessive love montage scored by Max Steiner and romantic leading men can acknowledge their bisexual tendencies. Right, Sam?"

Sam winked and launched into a spirited medley of Broadway show tunes.

"Here's my suggestion: You two lovebirds take the stolen letters of transport. Sam and I will take over Rick's. We could make it into a cabaret kind of thing, maybe a few corner booths, little umbrellas in the drinks—"

"Why, Lazlo! How courageous of you to declare openly your bisexuality, thus freeing us all from living lives of quiet desperation, in denial of our true selves!" exclaimed Ilsa.

"Come on," said Rick, holding up his drink. "Let's toast. Here's to Lazlo, to Sam, and to the beginning of a beautiful relationship."

6

Romeo and Juliet

*(Or, When You Assume You Make an ASS Out of
U and ME)*

PROLOGUE

[Enter]

CHORUS:

From forth the fatal loins of two foes

A pair of star-crossed lovers might take their life,

For misadventured piteous overthroes

could with their death bury their parents' strife.

Of course, all this could've been eas'ly o'er leaped

Had said lovers told their respective families of origin to go
get bleeped.

[*Exit*]

ACT I, SCENE I

[*Enter Romeo and Juliet*]

ROMEO:

O, she doth teach the torches to burn bright!

It seems she hangs upon the cheek of night

As a rich jewel in an Ethiop's ear.

(Not that I consider her a mere ornament,

for she is a fully rounded and equal potential partner of choice.)

Beauty too rich for use, for earth too dear.

(Although I do not mean to imply

that she is an idealized vision of unattainable female perfection,

but rather a woman perfect in her imperfections

that make her uniquely herself,

giving her a natural beauty of the spirit that radiates

from within.)

Did my heart love 'til now? Forswear it, sight!

For I ne'er saw true beauty 'til this night.

[*Romeo crosses to Juliet and takes her by the hand*]

I must profane with my most unworthy lips

this holy shrine with a tender kiss
and ask you gently, tell me, miss,
what's a fair maid like you doing in a place like this?
JULIET:
Good pilgrim, you do wrong your lips too much, methinks.
What do you say? You, me, my place? After-dinner drinks?
(Of course, I refer to nonalcoholic refreshments,
for we lovers have not yet attained the age of consent.)
ROMEO:
Tell me, sweet angel, lady so fine,
What is thy name? What is thy sign?
JULIET:
Good pilgrim, they call me Juliet
and my sign is Capulet.
ROMEO:
Are you a Capulet? O, dear account
My life is my foe's debt,
I can't take you out
for I am a Montague
or in the Broadway musical version, a Jet.
JULIET:
[gasping in horror]
My only love, sprung from my only hate!

Too early seen unknown, and known too late.

ROMEO:

Say what? You lost me there.

JULIET:

In other words, dude, this totally sucks! Anon! Hie thee,
    away!

[Exeunt]

ACT II, SCENE I

[Juliet's balcony. Enter Juliet above at her window. Romeo advances]

ROMEO:

But soft, what light through yonder window breaks?

It is the east, and Juliet is the sun.

Arise, fair sun, and kill the envious moon.

(Metaphorically speaking, naturally,

for I certainly do not condone violence in any form,

being a lover, not a fighter.)

It is my lady, O, it is my love.

JULIET:

Oh Romeo, Romeo, wherefore art thou, Romeo?

Deny thy father and refuse thy name

or if thou wilt not, be but sworn, my love

and I'll no longer be a Capulet.

You can just call me Juliet.

Maybe Juliet, exclamation point,

Or the Maiden Formerly Known as Juliet Capulet.

ROMEO:

Call me but love,

and I'll be new baptized.

Henceforth I never will be Montague.

The kids at school were always teasing me about my name
    anyhoo.

JULIET:

Swear?

ROMEO:

Lady, by yonder blessed moon I vow.

JULIET:

[coyly]

The inconstant moon? That monthly changes in her orb

and brings me PMS? 'Tis a fine vow that!

ROMEO:

By the sun then.

JULIET:

[even more coyly still]

Whose UV rays

doth rob my skin

of its youthful elasticity
and all essential emollients?

ROMEO:

Methinks though dost have issues
regarding the aging process.
Dost thou fear I shall leave you
when the bloom is off the rose?
A rose at any age doth smell as sweet.

JULIET:

Although we are only thirteen,
I am ready for a lifetime commitment,
aren't thou?

ROMEO:

By my troth,
I fear not the "C" word.
I do pledge my steadfast fidelity
and unflagging, noninvasive support for you
in any life endeavor.

JULIET:

Cool.
But now, I must retire for the night.
Parting is such sweet sorrow
that I should say good-bye
'til it be morrow.

ROMEO:

Wilt thou leave me so unsatisfied?

JULIET:

What satisfaction canst thou have tonight?

I don't put out on the first date.

The ring first,

buddy.

ROMEO:

[apologetic]

You shall have it at the morrow's first light.

[Exeunt]

ACT III, SCENE I

[The chambers of the ghostly Friar Laurence. Enter Chorus]

CHORUS:

So the next morning, when the sun stood tiptoe on yonder
    rosy hill

the lovers were joined in a secret holy pact by the ghostly
    Friar Laurence.

But ere the first nightingale sang her nightly hymn

Romeo did insist on going out with the boys one last time

and over an ill-fated game of draughts slew Juliet's cousin Tybalt,

Causing Romeo to be banished henceforth from Verona

and never again to play draughts for money.

And that very night did Juliet's father betroth her to the
    County Paris,
For this was thirteenth-century Verona
and he did not respect a woman's right to choose.
Desperate, Juliet approached the ghostly father in his
    chambers
and begged him remedy her wretched state
For she had not yet learned to heed the call of her inner voice
whose wisdom surely would have hatched a better plan than
    the cockamamie one that follows.

[Exeunt]

FRIAR LAURENCE:

Go home, be merry, give consent to marry Paris.
Take thou this vial, being then in bed . . . Look you, alone
and this distilling liquor drink thou of
(it being nonalcoholic as well as completely free of additives,
preservatives, artificial colors or flavors)
when presently through all thy veins shall run a cold and
    drowsy humour
and thou shalt appear as dead.
Thou shalt be borne to that ancient vault where all the dead
    Capulets lie.
In the meantime shall Romeo by my letters know our drift

and hither shall he come and will watch thy waking

And that very night shall Romeo bear thee hence to Mantua

Or any other place where you mutually decide to embark

    upon your life's journey.

JULIET:

[*who follows the advice of the male medical establishment without a second thought, Our Bodies, Ourselves not having yet been written*]

Give me, O give me. Tell not me of fear.

[*Exeunt*]

ACT IV

[*Enter Chorus at the Capulet tomb where Juliet lies in state, unconquered by death.*]

CHORUS:

And so did Juliet drink of the sinister apothecary

made for her by the ghostly father,

and as the roses in her lips and cheeks

faded to wanny ashes,

and her eyes' windows fell,

she dreamed of Romeo,

who would surely come to fetch her

ere she died, strangled in her family tomb,

being somewhat phobic about decomposition generally

and really claustrophobic.
Everything would have gone according to plan
had only the messenger
sent by the ghostly father
to inform Romeo of the ruse
admitted that he had taken a wrong turn
somewhere around Padua
and needed directions,
or if Friar Laurence
had broken down and paid extra
for Next-Day Air service.
Unfortunately, neither thing happened,
and when Romeo learned
of his beloved Juliet's death
from his friend Benvolio,
who was a hell of a nice guy
but chronically premature,
he rushed to her graveside,
grief stricken,
believing her actually dead.
ROMEO:
O my love, my wife, Death that hath suck'd the honey of thy
    breath,

Hath no power yet upon thy beauty: Thou art not conquer'd.
Here will I remain. Here will I set up my everlasting rest.
Eyes, look your last! Arms, take your last embrace!
and lips, seal with a righteous kiss a dateless bargain to
    engrossing death!
[Romeo lifts the poison to his lips]
Waaaaaait a minute.
Perhaps I am falling prey
to the impetuous romanticism
about which Juliet warned me.
Hasn't she always told me
that when you *assume*,
you make an *ass* out of *u* and *me*?
Maybe I should take some time out,
make a few inquiries
as to the true nature
of these seemingly tragic events.
Perhaps there is a way
to turn my scars into stars
which just isn't presenting itself
in the moment.
Maybe I should adopt the lotus position
and chant my personal mantra.

JULIET:

[*moaning groggily*]

O Romeo, Romeo, where art thou, Romeo?

ROMEO:

[*overjoyed*]

Here my love! Then thou art alive.

JULIET:

Aye good pilgrim, what thoughtest thou,

that I would leave you before the honeymoon?

Now bear me hence from this vile nest of contagion

for I fear for my sinus condition,

and I have a real thing

about tight subterranean spaces

peopled with the corpses of my kinsmen.

ROMEO:

I shall and gladly too, with my sword raised triumphantly in
exaltation.

JULIET:

Oh happy dagger, here is thy sheath.

ROMEO:

Oo la la!

[*Exeunt omnes*]

7

Legends of the Fall

(Or, My Heroes Have Always Been Outlaws with Good Hair)

ome people hear their own inner voices with great clearness, and they live by what they hear. Such people become crazy, but they become legends, especially if they happen to be a cherub-faced Midwestern male ingenue with a mischievous grin, good bone structure, and a washboard stomach, like, say, Brad Pitt.

Tristan Ludlow was born in the moon of the falling leaves. It was a terrible winter—his mother almost died bringing him into this world, but I think I speak for a generation of women when I say it would have been well worth the sacrifice. His father, the colonel, brought him to me, and I wrapped him in a bearskin, which contrasted fetchingly with his popsicle blue eyes.

As he grew into a man I taught him the great joy of the kill, when the hunter cuts out the warm heart, holding it in his hands, setting the spirit free. Of course, I don't mean kill in the literal masculist sense of the word: slaughtering innocent animals has no place in the definition of modern, noninterventionist male hero- ism, especially since whole grains and legumes provide the essen- tial amino acids found in red meat. What I meant was that we must metaphorically slay the demons that cause us to wallow in guilt over events beyond our control, like, say, world wars, and that prevent us from taming our inner bear.

Unfortunately, Tristan liked red meat. But what do you expect from a white, Anglo-Saxon, Protestant, early-twentieth-century frontiersman? And besides, you don't get to wear leather chaps or swing a lasso when you harvest legumes.

Anyway, I have these letters, many letters—but I am One Stab, a venerated elder of the Cree nation who has counted coup on hundreds of my enemies, and I refuse to read English because I consider it a spiritually bankrupt language invented by a society of white men drunk on expansionism and beef by-products. So you read them. The whole story is written here.

Colonel Ludlow had three sons, but Tristan was the one with star quality: perhaps it was his irreverent spirit; perhaps it was the bear growling deep within him, or perhaps it was his good hair. The older brother, Alfred, had piercing blue eyes and fairly good cheekbones but didn't have the stuff legends are made of. Samuel, the youngest, was an idealist with a penchant for botany, ballads, and befriending marooned extraterrestrials. Samuel did manage a certain wide-eyed, boyish charm, however, despite his mawkish sentimentality, that attracted the attentions of a raven-haired beauty from back East named Susannah. That spring, Susannah and Samuel became engaged and Susannah made the difficult journey to the Ludlow Ranch in the sweeping, epic, cinemascopic wilds of Calgary.

As Tristan rode up over the hillside, however, looking very Viper Room, his sunny locks blowing in the first gentle winds of summer as a rousing soundtrack swelled in the distance, Susannah quickly realized that her young fiancé paled in comparison to his brother, whose golden good looks and amber backlighting stole every scene.

"So this is Tristan," said Susannah, watching transfixed as a puckish smile crept across Tristan's legendary cheekbones.

"Miss Fincannon, it's a pleasure to meet you. I hope you and Ugly here find every happiness together," said Tristan, allowing a come-hither fire to kindle seductively in his bottomless bedroom eyes before wrestling both brothers to the ground, proving that not only was he better billed and better looking, but better coordinated than any frontiersman this side of the Continental Divide.

In the days that followed, Susannah settled into life at the ranch, learning to pick peas, play tennis, rope cattle, and hit a target dead on at thirty paces, all without breaking a nail. At night, she gazed longingly from her bedroom window at Tristan taming wild mares with a sensual tenderness that hinted at a knack for simultaneous orgasm.

One evening, Samuel announced that he was going off to war. He had been taken in by pro-war rhetoric and was too dense to realize that once he was out of the picture, the next mare that Tristan tamed would be Susannah.

"The Germans broke through at Armentierres," said Samuel. "The entire British third core is trapped in the Belgian lowlands. This is a turning point in the history of the world, and it's my duty as a symbol of early-twentieth-century blind militaristic male heroism to enlist immediately."

"But son," said the colonel, "why must you go now, in the summer of the red grass, to fight a war against an enemy you've never seen, to avenge the deaths of a couple of distant cousins who have never even so much as sent us a Christmas card? Don't you realize that this war is nothing but a metaphor for man's inhumanity to man, as well as a graphic illustration of the dangerous consequences of well-intentioned but misguided nationalist sentiment?"

"I'm going, too," Alfred interrupted. "I know that I'm a second-billed brother who must ultimately come to represent the futility of all earthly gain and the corruptive nature of political power, but that doesn't happen until the second act, and I've got to have something to do for the next twenty scenes." Together, he and Samuel stomped up to their bedrooms to prepare for war. The colonel also stomped off to bed, lest the stroke that would one day reduce him to a camp combination of King Lear and Helen Keller strike him that very night.

"Please, don't let him go," wept Susannah, burying her stricken face in that haunting hollow where Tristan's prominent jaw line met his graceful yet well-corded and virile neck.

"I'll go with him and take care of him. Shhh. Shhh," whispered Tristan into Susannah's ear, taming her tears as she had seen him tame the wild horses, and suddenly Susannah understood why those mares were so willing to be ridden. Unfortunately, just as Tristan was about to climb into the saddle, Alfred entered the room. Alas, Tristan dismounted, without having taught Susannah to canter.

The next morning, the brothers rode off to war, where Samuel, gripped by antiquated and naïve notions about the glory of battle, volunteered to run up over every fortified hill in the Fatherland. Tristan had vowed to protect his brother without any thought of his own personal safety and, regardless, could kick the crap out of any ten Krauts this side of the Marne. He kept his brother safe for a time. But Samuel, who couldn't even look macho smoking a cigarette while basking in a post-combat afterglow, eventually managed to get himself nerve-gassed, blinded, entangled in barbed wire, and shot fifty-seven times by an automatic machine gun.

"Samuel! Samuel!" bellowed Tristan, hugging his brother to his smooth, totally buffed breast. "You're doing good, Samuel. We're going home. The purity of my fraternal love will surely save you from the nerve gas, the barbed wire, and all fifty-seven rounds of automatic gunfire."

Unfortunately, assault weapons turned out to be mightier than the power of Tristan's screen presence, a fact that proved too much for Tristan's sensitive and vulnerable but nevertheless potent and steely spirit to bear. He cursed God, cut his brother's heart out, and sent it home encased in paraffin, painted his face with his brother's blood, scalped fifty-seven Germans (one for every bullet), and returned home. He rode up over the crest of the hill like an emblem of the doomed beauty of youth itself, his golden hair blowing in the last languorous breezes of summer, while dressed in a loose, belted, Calvin Klein–inspired ensemble that hugged his slim, virile loins just so.

But not even the embrace of his father, the colonel, or the knowing eyes of his spiritual father, One Stab, or Susannah's devoted affection could resurrect Tristan's frail and wounded though indomitable and adamantine spirit. Tristan was anguished, tormented by personal demons, and at odds with a God that had blessed him with the face of an angel and the hair of a Breck girl but cursed him with an macho ego that caused him to feel responsible for all external events despite his limited capacity to influence them. Had he taken a hint from One Stab, perhaps he could have connected with a more feminine spirituality that recognizes the powerlessness of man over nature and instead emphasizes harmony with the environment. But all that red meat had taken its toll and so he descended into a kind of madness. He grew despondent and remote from his loved ones. He was overcome by guilt and testosterone, and his masculine impulses caused him to withdraw and repress his negative feelings in a most unhealthy manner. He had terrible dreams and attacked Susannah in the night, mistaking her for some imagined enemy. He slugged a bartender. He rode erratically. He did not neatly trim his beard.

Was it the bear's voice he heard deep within, growling

low in dark, secret places, or a clogged vessel in his brain caused by excessive consumption of polyunsaturated fats? Whichever, no one was completely surprised when Tristan saddled up his mare one morning prepared to ride out of their lives forever. Susannah followed him out to the corral, where he was caressing his favorite nag.

"Were you going to say good-bye?" asked Susannah, her face aglow with the need to nurture. "Tristan? How long will you be gone?"

"Not long . . . a few months," said Tristan, avoiding eye contact, not because he was cowardly or evasive, but because his brave yet fragile heart was threatening to break in two.

"Can't I make it better for you?" asked Susannah. She moved closer to him, placing a tentative hand in that miraculous meadow where the swell of his buttocks met the small of his back. Susannah did this not because she felt in anyway responsible for his leaving—she knew that the issues that prevented him from forming an enduring emotional bond with another were his own responsibility—but because she could see that Tristan was about to cry, and that always got her hot.

"If we'd had a child, or if I were pregnant, would you still be going?"

"Yes. Are you?"

"No, but give me a chance," said Susannah. She unbuttoned his shirt and began to trace with her tongue the creases in Tristan's washboard stomach.

"Don't do that," said Tristan. "A little to the left, now to the right, now faster."

"I'll wait for you. However long it takes. I'll wait for you forever."

"Hold it," said Tristan.

"I am holding it," said Susannah.

"No, I mean, hold everything."

"You're getting very demanding lately, do you know that? I've put up with your being somewhat self-involved sexually, because, well, after all, you are emblematic of the doomed beauty of youth, but I do have my limits, and if you think I'm just going to hang around here in the sweeping, epic cinemascopic wilds of Calgary while you run off and hunt rare zoological specimens, you better think again. I'll go out of my gourd up here. They don't even have cable!"

Tristan sighed and gazed soulfully into the distance. For a long time he could not speak, but then suddenly, like the sun rising after a long winter's night, a slow smile crept across his well-sculpted face and he reached personal epiphany.

"Listen to me," said Tristan, "It is true that the bear within is growling, urging me to board a square rigger and head for exotic locales no white man has ever seen before. It is true that at night I dream of becoming a hunter. I have this irresistible desire to cover my body with ash, to wear a boar's tusk necklace carefully crafted by a Javanese warrior, and to sleep with Tahitian teenagers two at a time. Then I long to cleanse myself, Christlike, in pure mountain pools. But I realize that I have promised myself to you, and even though I still have a boy's urge to wander and indulge in the joys of the kill, I am a man now. I have responsibilities, and any decisions I make about my future must also include you. So, where would you like to go on vacation?"

Susannah's heart soared with joy. The tongue-tracing thing worked every time.

"Well, I did get a great-looking brochure from the Fiji Club Med. We can make a reservation in the morning but first, why don't you go get the lunge line and teach me how to canter?"

They were last seen in the tropics, wearing his and her boar's tusk necklaces, sipping Mai Tais alongside a pure mountain pool on an uncharted desert isle, somewhere in the borderland between this world and the other. It was a good vacation.

8

The Great Gatsby

(Or, What Is He Compensating For?)

atsby lived at West Egg, in a factual imitation of some hotel de ville in Normandy with a tower on one side spanking new under a thin beard of raw ivy and a marble swimming pool and more than forty acres of lawn and garden. Gatsby's mansion was a monument to the consumerist amoral aestheticism inherent in the dehumanizing mechanisms of the modern industrial complex and also probably a dick thing—but I'm getting ahead of myself.

Across the courtesy bay, glittering along the water were the white palaces of fashionable East Egg, including the mansion of Tom and Daisy Buchanan, an unpretentious couple living quietly in their understated villa, which had a fourteen-car garage, two swimming pools, and a moat. They were card-carrying aristocrats who did not need architectural compensations to make up for their lack of breeding or sexual endowments. It was just that they didn't believe in skimping and the thought of life with only one swimming pool was unimaginable—and everyone needed a moat.

One day at lunch on the verandah that overlooked the second swimming pool at the eastern edge of the moat, Daisy Buchanan, a woman painfully at odds with the natural elements, not because they had a tendency to clash with her china pattern but because they reminded her of the unnatural life she was living as a full-fledged member of the landed aristocracy, turned to her husband, vexed.

"Darling Tom, couldn't you please, please, do something about that dreadful sun? It's shining all over my table and absolutely obliterating the jewel tones in my Harlequin Limoges, not to mention the fact that it is highlighting my undeserved and overblown sense of entitlement with its relentless light devoid of all forgiving shadow."

"I'm sorry, Buttercup. Perhaps we could get a parasol that would cover the entire house as well as all forty-seven acres of landscaped garden, both swimming pools, your overblown sense of entitlement, and the moat, except for the portion with the Japanese water lilies, because don't they need light or something to bloom?"

Daisy sighed. "I keep waiting and waiting for that one day a year when those lilies bloom, and then I miss it, kind of like I missed out on being a proletarian heroine like *la femme Liberté* with my arm upraised and my left breast exposed as I challenge a decadent and tyrannical monarchy. Instead I was born with all of these dreadful millions and have had to spend my life draped in yards of this horrible yellow silk chiffon, which does not breathe at all and, in case you hadn't noticed, we are living in an age before air-conditioning. And I never get to expose my breasts in public. Life is so unjust."

She drew a long draught of her martini and wistfully recalled the determined face of her proletariat lover, lost to her so many years before. Then, her countenance grew suddenly dark.

"Tear them up. The lot of them. I'm sick of them, sick of them, do you hear me? Sick, sick, sick, sick!"

Tom clucked at her in sympathy. "There, there, Petunia. Try to bear up. I know these are difficult times, considering the precariousness of the severely inflated domestic marketplace, the vast gulf separating rich from poor that threatens to bring about class revolt, the winds of oppression gathering off the shores and whipping up a tidal wave of change that will one day inundate our tranquil shores, costing us our inno-cence, our sense of order, our isolationism, as well as the sec-ond swimming pool and probably our maintenance contract on the moat, but we simply must carry on."

"You know what I can't stand about you, Tom? You are socially unaware and hopelessly bourgeois. Don't you know there are people out there without moats?" Daisy sighed again and gazed disconsolately across the courtesy bay to West Egg, where those poor, unfortunate, moatless masses who didn't know any better than to stir and not shake lived, and won-dered whatever became of her handsome, heroic Jay Gatsby. Had he, by some Marxist miracle, found a dry corner in which to huddle as he planned the workers' revolt?

Daisy, who had been myopic from birth, did not see the lone figure gazing back at her through a pair of high-powered German field glasses. Yet even if she had seen those mecha-nized eyes, focused just below her diaphanous yellow chiffon veil at her fashionably diminutive décolletage, she would never have guessed that they belonged to her lost love.

Jay Gatsby cut a lithe and laconic silhouette against the lavender evening sky. There was something gorgeous about him, and not just because he had windswept, flaxen hair, a killer jawline, well-sculpted cheekbones, and a drop-dead dimple, but because there was in him a heightened sensitivity to the promises of life, an extraordinary gift for hope, a romantic readiness, and a prodigious trouser bulge (which may have been his billfold—obviously another dick thing).

Gatsby sighed as he placed his hand deep into his left pocket—now, you *know* that was a dick thing—but who could begrudge him his twilight fantasies? He had lived a life of utter isolation, cut off from all but the most superficial inter-course with others, so absorbed was he in his private romance with the past. This was an indication of a deep-seated fear of intimacy, as well as an anxiety-based rigidity that prevented him from bonding with an equal partner in a mutually sup-portive relationship. Clearly, he was sublimating his need for love, as well as his wishes for a larger male member, into a lav-ish, life-long spending spree, hence, the overstated, neo-Louis Quatorze villa filled with unwanted hangers-on.

Gatsby hosted many grand parties that summer in his blue gardens, where men and girls came and went like moths among the whisperings, and the champagne, and the stars. On weekends his Rolls-Royce became an omnibus bearing revel-ers to and from the city between nine in the morning and long past midnight, because although a bootlegger, he was a man with firm convictions about carpooling and believed that friends don't let friends drive drunk.

Gatsby appeared to take no pleasure in his guests, partially because at every party at least twelve people wound up either dancing with lampshades on their heads or passing out on his hand-chiseled, imported Italian Carrara marble powder room floor in various stages of deshabillé, but also because, unbeknownst to all of us, his main purpose in hosting these fêtes was to entice Daisy Buchanan to make her way across the bay to pay him a visit.

If only he had just dropped by one day for some herbal tea and petits fours while Daisy's husband was out, explained to her how he had been unable to resolve his issues stemming from their miscommunication years before, and asked for closure, he would have saved a fortune in catering bills. Instead, Gatsby flaunted his money, which Daisy, upon arriving at his palace that night, assumed was a dick thing.

"What hideous Doric columns!" Daisy said to Tom. "You know, the Dorics were horrible to their workers, and they weren't very well hung. Why do you think their entire philosophy of architecture is centered around these massive phallic symbols? If I've said it once, I've said it a thousand times, the history of the patriarchal oligarchy is not a pretty one. Tom, stop running your hands up and down that column and get me a drink."

"Right away, Rhododendron," said Tom, trotting off in the direction of the cocktail table.

Gatsby, pale as death, with his hands plunged like weights in his trouser pockets, was standing in a puddle of water, glaring tragically at Daisy.

"Daisy?" He choked, and then laughed artificially, and leaned back in a strained counterfeit of perfect ease, even of boredom, which is a typical male reaction to sudden, unexpected emotional vulnerability.

"Jay Gatsby?" Daisy exclaimed, her robin's egg–blue eyes widening in amazement.

"How do you like my factual imitation of some hotel de ville in Normandy with a tower on one side spanking new under a thin beard of raw ivy and a marble swimming pool and more than forty acres of lawn and garden?" Jay Gatsby said grandly, displaying his financial success as if it were the true measure of a man's worth, in a typical gesture of materialistic male posturing.

"Oh Jay," Daisy whispered, tragically, tears streaking her face, "you've changed so. And you don't even have a moat?"

"It's on order," said Jay, believing that she was impressed with his newfound wealth, when in actuality she was appalled at his horrible taste in interior design and was wondering what had become of that trouser bulge that he now had to resort to Doric architecture.

"Come," said Gatsby as he led her upstairs, through period

bedrooms swathed in rose and lavender silk and vivid with new flowers, through dressing rooms and pool rooms and bathrooms with sunken baths. He threw open a hulking patent cabinet, took out a pile of shirts, and began throwing them one by one before her. There were shirts of sheer linen and thick silk and fine flannel which lost their folds as they fell and covered the table in many-colored disarray. The soft, rich heap mounted higher—shirts with stripes and scrolls and plaids in coral and apple green and lavender and faint orange with monograms of Indian blue.

Suddenly, with a strained sound, Daisy bent her head into the shirts and began to cry stormily. "Oh Jay, so many hideous shirts. I've never seen so many hideously repulsive, overstated, loud, outdated, and badly tailored shirts in all my life. It makes me so terribly sad and, also, slightly nauseated. Who told you you could carry off pastels? Didn't I warn you years ago that you must avoid primary colors and pastels because you are an autumn? Don't you know that lavender washes you out, making your eyes look piggy and your lips thin and fluid-less?"

"But Daisy," Gatsby protested, "I thought you left me for Tom because, next to your father, he had more pastel shirts than anyone in the Hamptons."

"Oh my darling, it was your misguided adherence to bourgeois values at the expense of your principles, which I so ardently shared, that deprived you of my love. What happened to all of our dreams about getting a small third-floor cold-water walk-up, wearing fetching berets while we liberate the masses and redistribute wealth? That was the man I wanted to marry, not some materialistically obsessed half man who has to compensate for his lack of virility through material possessions and phallic architecture. Oh Jay, what happened to your ideals, what happened to that brave heart, that heroic soul, that utopian vision, that bulge in your trousers?"

An expression of bewilderment had come back into Gatsby's face, as though a faint doubt had occurred to him as to the quality of his present happiness. He realized the colossal vitality of his illusion. He had thrown himself into it with a creative passion, decking it out with every bright feather and phallic symbol that drifted his way. No amount of fire or freshness or Freudian symbolism can challenge what a man will store up in his ghostly heart.

"Daisy, I realize now that I've been a fool hiding behind hollow symbols of patriarchal potency when really all I ever truly needed was right here in your arms, and in my pants. My darling, you have helped me to regain my manhood, and it's throbbing as we speak."

He adjusted himself a little, and in Daisy's eyes shone the

realization that that was no billfold in his pocket; he was happy to see her.

Jay liquidated his fortune and donated it all to the ACLU. Daisy filed for divorce from Tom, who was carrying on with one of Gatsby's Doric columns, and she and Jay began a new life as comrades for the cause. They moved into a small, drafty, cockroach-infested, moatless third-floor cold-water walk-up in Greenwich Village . . . which was definitely not a dick thing.

9

The Thorn Birds

(Or, Father Ralph's Personal Reformation)

t was four in the morning when Father Ralph got through the last gate and into the Home Paddock. All through the drive he had willed his mind to blankness; he wouldn't let himself think, not of the great tragedies that had befallen his dear Meggie, for which he hoped to comfort her, nor of her sad countenance, her waiflike hunger for healing, for spiritual nourishment, for love, for his mouth that wanted more and more of her, and his tongue, which traveled down her shoulders, smooth, smoother, and glossier than satin, toward the small peaks of her supple, pouting breasts. No, he did not think of these things—really, he didn't. Instead, he opened his eyes and mind to the night, to the ghostly silver of dead trees standing lonely in the gleaming grass, which had absolutely no phallic, Freudian significance whatsoever, to the batting averages of the starting lineup of the Sydney baseball team, to the heart-of-darkness shadows cast by stands of timber, to the full moon riding the heavens like an airy bubble.

He stopped the car and got out, walked to a wire fence, and leaned on its tautness, which did not remind him at all of the way her thigh muscles, so beautifully sculpted by a lifetime on horseback, gripped the saddle as she worked the stockhorses at Drogheda, gently coaxing the beasts into submission. No, he didn't think of that either. He breathed in the gums and the bewitching aroma of wildflowers. He stood in the warm spring rain, thinking how it ought to be a cold shower like his mentor Archbishop Vittoria Scarbanza di Contini-Verchese had recommended. The land was so beautiful, so pure, so indifferent to the fates of the creatures who presumed to rule it. Yes, the Australian outbackers might put their hands to it and massage it gently with elegant, refined fingers smoothed in service to the Lord yet strong with forbidden knowledge, coaxing the virgin landscape into mature blossoming, but in the long run it ruled them.

Father Ralph stepped onto the verandah, wet and muddy in riding clothes and oilskins.

"Oh, Father, Father!" cried Meggie, flinging open the screen door, her ashes-of-roses gown fluttering delicately behind her, her bountiful red-gold tresses bouncing with perky vitality, her dark, injured eyes, doelike in their simple innocence, flashing joy and newly burgeoning, intuitive, intelligent, and autonomous womanhood. She embraced him.

"Oh my poor, wee Meggie," he said, taking her cold hands in his wet ones firmly. "I'm wet, darling Meggie. You'll get soaked."

"I'm already soaked, Father," she said. "Come inside by the roaring fire."

Father Ralph's jaw dropped and he followed Meggie inside, where he fell back into a chair. Meggie smiled and crawled into his arms, pillowing her head in his dripping lap, and closing her eyes. Father Ralph gulped and said no more, but held her and rocked her as if she were a baby, until the heat of the fire (which bore no resemblance whatsoever to any fires of passion burning in his breast) partially dried his shirt and hair and he felt some of the stiffness drain from her. He put his hand beneath her chin, tilted her head until she looked up at him, and, without thinking, kissed her. Fingers steady, she unbuttoned his damp shirt and peeled it off his arms, pulled it free of his straining breeches. Meggie suddenly gasped. It was big, it was ugly, it was purple, and it stretched all the way from beneath his ribcage to that grassy knoll just beneath his solar plexus. Her head went down.

"Oh, my. Gee, that bruise, uh, I must've hurt myself preparing for mass this morning. You know, the baptismal font is at a very awkward height—"

A trail of gentle kisses was heading south while her palms headed north, up his chest toward his shoulders, moving with a sensuousness that staggered him.

"I don't think there's any internal bleeding or anything, I mean, I can barely even feel it now. I was just in such a hurry to make sure you were all right," he said, wholly concerned with her spiritual well-being in this time of great tragedy, for he had journeyed far to comfort her.

He drew a sharp breath suddenly. "God, Meggie, don't. I'm a priest." He pulled her head away, but somehow all he succeeded in doing was having her back in his arms, a snake coiled tightly about his will, strangling it. Pain was forgotten. Church was forgotten. God was forgotten, along with the names and batting averages of the entire starting lineup of the Sydney baseball team. He found her mouth, forced it open hungrily, wanting more and more of her. Mortality pressed down on him, a great weight crushing his soul, liberating the bitter dark wine of his senses in a sudden flood. He wanted to weep as the last of his desire trickled away, and he wrenched her arms from about his wretched body.

"Meggie, what have you done to me? What might you do to me if I let you? I can't."

"Can't? What do you mean, can't? I'm just getting warmed up."

"Meggie, I love you and I always will, but I just can't . . . I'm a priest."

"Listen Ralph, I understand you're a little conflicted about this Catholicism-slash-oath-of-celibacy thing, but I've got real problems. A drought has gripped the entire country-side, plunging my family into abject poverty. A flash fire has claimed the life of my father, and my favorite brother has just been crushed by a wild boar he inadvertently roused while firing a warning shot to the rest of the party that was searching for my father, who had already been consumed in the blaze. I have just learned that my other favorite brother, Frank, is serving a life sentence in a London prison. The sheep are dying, the wool is ruined, the kangas are moving close to the neighborhoods, there's some strange virus affecting the rabbits that could be germ warfare, and, to top things off, I have a cold and distant mother who can't stand the sight of me because it reminds her of her own disappointed girlhood. So don't cry to me about your philosophical dilemmas. I've got needs here, pal."

"Meggie, please try to understand, I'll be fully vested in five years, and they say I'm a shoe-in for archbishop, and I look so good in a red cassock cinched around my manly but lithe torso. Please, you've got to forget me."

"Now Ralph, you know as well as I do that that just isn't possible. If we try to deny our true feelings they only come back to haunt us later. Remember, we become what we ignore, and what we do not overcome ultimately overcomes us. If I let you go off now without addressing your inner feelings, they will come back to haunt you, probably as the ghost of an illegitimate and unacknowledged son, who will make the same mistakes that you have, ultimately costing him his life, and me what little love I have left for you. I'll be filled with bitterness and ultimately deny God, you'll be filled with doubt, never really knowing whether you love God more than me, and you will be walking around for most of your life with the worst case of blue balls this side of the international date line."

There was a wail, the sound of a soul passing between the portals of hell. Ralph de Bricassart fell forward out of the chair, and wept, huddled on the crimson carpet.

"Meggie, what shall I do?" he wept, his face hidden in his folded arms, his hands clutching at his hair.

"For goodness' sake, Ralph. Just become a Methodist. You can nix the sexual guilt trip but still be a vessel filled with God, hearing those awed breaths and knowing the power you have over every soul in the congregation. I mean, the Methodists have a pension plan, don't they? And they've got much better hymns."

"Hmmm," said Ralph. Then, suddenly filled with hope and new insight, he arose, pulling Meggie to his breast and gazing thankfully to the heavens, before drinking in her eyes. "Of course you are right. You have shown me the light, my darling, and I realize now that my escape into the Catholic church was not motivated by my love of God but by an overweening ambition and my type-A tendencies, which place power and position over love and family, relationships, and connectedness."

"Oh Ralph, can you really rid yourself of those masculist values and embrace what is truly important in life?"

"Yes, my darling, for you have given me the insight and emotional courage. Meggie, I want you to be my wife. I want to have a son with you whom we can raise according to the Montessori method, free from restrictive supervisory structures, so that he will never make the same mistakes I have. We'll escape this parched, unforgiving land and move to a nice suburban split-level on a corner lot somewhere in the midwestern United States. We can build a life together. For you I can give up my hollow ambition and become a humble, suburban minister. Our children shall all wear glasses, and you shall coordinate the pancake breakfasts and spearhead Vacation Bible School. For you I shall learn to sing 'What a Friend We Have in Jesus.'"

"You would do all that for us, Ralph?" asked Meggie.

"Of course, but do you think the congregation would mind if I wore my red cassock on occasion? It looks so swell on me."

"I'm sure they won't Ralph," said Meggie encouragingly. "And if they do, there's always the Unitarians."

IO

Samson and Delilah

(Or, Even God Gets His Ends Trimmed)

s the angel of the Lord had promised, so did the wife of Manoah give birth to Samson. He grew and the Lord blessed him with great wisdom, great strength, and long, luxuriant locks with a natural wave and golden highlights and a peek-a-boo cowlick that fell over his left eye just so. Buffed and coiffed as he was, the young Samson really wowed the neighborhood maidens, as well as a number of fellow countrymen, particularly those who resided in renovated flats above tony cafés in the West Village. He was a leader among men, and all respected him, except for the Philistines, who were pea green with envy, being, generally speaking, a follically challenged lot.

In return for these blessings, God asked that Samson avoid strong drink, unclean food, and trendy hairstylists, in particular Jean Louis David, because God had a thing about that uneven, angular Eurotrash look, although he did give permission for a few wispy bangs and a little layering in the front, just for shape.

For twenty years did Samson rule the Israelites and obey God's law, remaining on a strict macrobiotic diet and avoiding blunt cuts. To fill his days he prayed religiously, berated infidels, spoke out against injustice, led his people, solved disputes among the Israelites, and regularly smote Philistines with the jawbone of an ass. This last indulgence in imperialist aggression was to become the hallmark of the Judeo-Christian tradition of which a loving, nurturing, and antiblunt-cut God would surely not approve. But after all, this was the Old Testament.

After a succession of unhappy, short-term relationships that perhaps could have been avoided if Samson had spent a little less time smiting and a little more time working through his issues, Samson met Delilah, a woman who brought Samson's walls tumbling down around him. Having established a mutually satisfying and supportive relationship, they chose to wed.

Years passed as Samson and Delilah worked together to

deepen the bonds of their intimacy. Each was careful to share, care, and validate each other, as well as to lovingly support the other in their individual challenges toward self-actualization. They also encouraged growth in specific problem areas. For example, Delilah knew that Samson had real issues surrounding his hair, which had by this time grown well beyond his shoulders and was beginning to look dull, limp, and lifeless. Samson, Delilah felt, needed to address his personal grooming conflicts, and get a deep-conditioning treatment, and maybe even one of those trendy new blunt cuts.

"Samson, darling," she suggested lovingly, making sure not to put him on the defensive because she knew this was a volatile subject. "Don't you think that you're about due for a haircut?"

Samson stiffened. "No, for therein resides my strength and it is my covenant with the Lord." He was obviously listening to his old tapes and was not open to new dialogue.

Exasperated at his rigidity, Delilah lost her patience. "Oh, for the love of Moab. Get with the times. This is 1000 B.C. You've had that haircut since the Moses administration. You know what your problem is? You hate change."

Samson looked at her accusingly. "Why dost though tempt me to turn from my God? He hath commanded me never to take a razor to my hair."

"Look, maybe God has a thing about blunt cuts, but surely even He gets his ends trimmed when they get straggly," she answered crossly. Then she touched his arm gently and spoke in a quiet, supportive tone. "Look, I know this is difficult for you, but remember how you fought me when I insisted that you get away from all those taupes and whites and put a little splash of color near your face? Remember how you said the Israelites could not respect a man who accessorized? You were wrong, weren't you, and yet you still insist on this totally outdated 'do of yours. Well, you know you've been slipping in the polls and one of these days someone's going to invent democracy and some upstart with a trendy haircut is going to capture the hearts of the Israelites and guess who will be out of a job? Look, sweetheart, just tell me, what are you afraid of? I know you have some control issues left over from your first marriage when your wife betrayed you to the Philistines—"

"Be silent, vile temptress—" Samson seethed.

"Don't you throw biblical epithets at me when I'm trying to have a discussion about difficult feelings! Why don't you face it? You have control issues. I mean, why do you think you feel compelled to run around smiting people with the bones of farm animals? Do you think that's healthy? Is slaying infidels a constructive way to work out your anger?"

Samson grew silent, remembering that Harriet Lerner

weekend on anger management and sensing that there might be a grain of truth in what his wife was saying to him. However, it was difficult for him to admit it, having internalized a sexist society's definition of appropriate male behavior.

Delilah continued, "You know what I think? I think your hair issue stems from an inability to trust women. I think it's time you let your vulnerable, feminine side shine through. Work with me, Samson. Tell me about the hair thing. What, you think that if I know your deepest secrets, if I know where you get your great strength, I'm going to tie you up, subdue you, and call in the Philistines?"

"Well . . ."

"Honey, I wouldn't hurt you for the world, or even eleven hundred shekels of silver. I may be a Philistine, but I'm your wife first and I would never let anyone tie you up and subdue you. Except me, of course," said Delilah, and she ran her hand down his chest suggestively.

Samson blushed, remembering those thongs of new leather, the seven ropes, and the whipped cream, which Delilah had introduced into their lovemaking. Those too, he had once believed, would sap his strength, but they had merely made him walk funny for a couple of days and had greatly enhanced their sex life.

"Delilah," he said softly. "Maybe I need to get in touch

with my feelings. Maybe I am falling into that typical male trap of mistaking my own opinion for God's truth. I think I need a little time out to meditate and get in touch with the burning bush within, for some guidance."

"You do that, darling, while I whip you up a kiwi-lecithin power shake," said Delilah.

And so Samson centered himself, and he heard the true voice of the Lord, who said, "Fear not, Samson, for our bond is a holy one, which cannot be blunt cut. The measure of a man's faith is not in his rigidity but in his ability to embrace change and the unfailing wisdom of his life partner. Bottom line: She's definitely hit the nail on the head, your hair is an embarrassment, and those split ends have got to go."

Thus enlightened and empowered, Samson booked an appointment with stylist José Eber, who is morally and aesthetically opposed to blunt cuts. Samson even reserved extra time for a manicure and a facial. Emerging from the salon, newly inspired, Samson saw Delilah waiting for him, with the new leather thongs, the seven ropes, and the whipped cream. That night, Samson and Delilah made love so passionately that the earth moved, felling several neighborhood structures including the temple of Dagon, wiping out yet another bogus masculist religion that discouraged creative lovemaking and bold hair statements.

II

Jane Eyre

(Or, Listening to Prozac)

Mr. Rochester must have been aware of the entrance of his new governess, but it appeared he was not in the mood to notice her, for he never lifted his head as she approached. Jane Eyre should have realized then that he had passive-aggressive tendencies that would one day escalate into a full-blown dance of deception, ultimately undermining the foundations of their intimacy and preventing fully satisfying coital relations, but she was too busy mentally constructing overly ornate, fustian, nineteenth-century, nonsensical, compound sentences to see past the nose on her face.

"Let Miss Eyre be seated," said Rochester, and there was

something in the forced stiff bow and the impatient yet formal tone that seemed further to express his inability to let down his defenses and bond with women, retreating instead into his own world, brooding over the past, watching *Star Trek* reruns, and surfing the Internet in search of cybersex. His harsh caprice laid Jane under no obligation. On the contrary, a decent quiescence under the freak of manner gave her the advantage, if only she could figure out how to phrase it without too many semicolons.

"So you are newly come from Lowell School. What do you think of that institution?" he asked, pressing her to reveal herself while he revealed nothing.

"I was near starved, tortured by the pompous and meddling Mr. Brocklehurst, exposed to typhus, and badly neglected in the areas of artistic expression and individual creativity. I was also beaten regularly and then was told I was being sent to hell for my disagreeable disposition. I suppose they thought I ought to be standing on my head naked spinning a pie plate on my toe and whistling Dixie at that treatment," she replied.

Mr. Rochester raised his formidable eyebrows. "Miss Eyre, you are of singular mind and temperament."

"You got that right. And by the way, I don't do windows," said Jane, laying firm boundaries right from the outset.

"What sort of furniture is in that mind of yours?" said Rochester, peering quizzically into her eyes, as if straining to decipher her mental motif.

"I'm sort of into rattan at present. It's light and easy to rearrange," she said. "Why? Are you considering redecorating? Because I don't do that either."

He shook his head and turned toward the window, away from her piercing gaze. "Jane, your soul sleeps; the shock is yet to be given which shall awaken it," he said, making the typical male mistake of underestimating his governess. "You think all existence lapses in as quiet a flow as that in which your youth has hitherto slid away. Floating on with closed eyes and muffled ears, you neither see the rocks bristling not far off in the bed of the flood nor hear the breakers boil at their base. But I tell you—and you mark my words—you will come some day to a craggy pass of the channel, where the whole of life's stream will be broken up into whirl and tumult, foam and noise: either you will be dashed to atoms on crag points or lifted up and borne on by some master wave into a calmer current—as I am now."

"I'm sorry, I dozed through most of that, but it's clear that somebody's got a little excess baggage he's carrying around and projecting onto others. And you seem awfully preoccupied with water images, which are, as you know, symbolic of an inability to deal with strong emotion as well as a reluctance to trust women, probably stemming from a conflicted relationship with your mother. Are you by any chance afraid of spiders?" said Jane, remembering that article about Freudian symbolism, which she had read in a recent issue of *Psychology for Governesses*, that linked arachnophobia with a subliminal fear of a powerful mother.

Mr. Rochester ground his teeth as he paced, obviously the precursor to a serious case of temporomandibular jaw syndrome.

"You really ought to be careful about grinding your teeth like that. It can create serious headaches and balance difficulties while flying, which would be a real problem for a guy like you who wants to travel constantly and avoid the personal demons lodged here at Thornfield," said Jane, aware of her employer's tendency toward avoidance behaviors.

Rochester arrested his step and struck his boot against the hard ground. Some hated thought seemed to have him it its grip and to hold him so tightly that he could not advance.

"Yes, yes, you are right," said he. "I have plenty of faults of my own, and I don't wish to palliate them, I assure you. I have a past existence, a series of deeds, a color of life to contemplate within my own breast. I was thrust on to a wrong tack at the age of one and twenty, and have never recovered the right course since." (Of course, had Rochester simply asked for directions at a gas station, perhaps he would have found his way 'ere this.)

Jane thought immediately of her young French charge, Miss Adele, who bore an uncanny resemblance to the master of the house, despite his claims that he and Adele's mother had been "just friends." Jane may have newly come from Lowell School, but she wasn't born yesterday, "What happened? So you knocked somebody up, right? That'll teach you to go courting without a condom."

He turned to her with wounded eyes (which Jane was a real sucker for, given her own victimized past, which compelled her to engage in codependent dynamics fueled by an unconscious repetition compulsion, despite the warnings against such behavior that she had read in an article in *Victim's Lifestyle*) and said, "I might have been very different; I might have been as good as you—wiser—almost as stainless. I envy your peace of mind, your clean conscience, your unpolluted memory, which no gush or bilge water has turned to fetid puddle."

"Hold on, buster," said Jane, unwilling to enable his avoidance behavior any longer or to comply with this overly romanticized and erroneous portrait of herself as some perfect embodiment of the nineteenth century's rendition of the waif look, which had never suited her, or anyone else for that matter. "You don't have an exclusive arrangement with tragedy. If you don't call being forced to stand on a stool in the pouring rain while some sadomasochistic headmaster threatens you with the fires of hell just on account of your economic status bilge water, than I don't know what is. And as for being stainless, it's only because I've forgiven myself. Let me tell you something. Guilt is a useless emotion. You start blaming yourself for every misstep, next thing you know, you're married to some half-crazed banshee who's burning your house down every time she slips out of her straitjacket and past the drunken, underpaid servant guarding her in the west wing. Is this ringing any bells here?"

Rochester merely shrugged, unwilling to reveal the secrets of either his inner psyche or the rubber guest room in the attic.

Months passed before Mr. Rochester finally broke down his defenses and addressed the issues head-on, not only because he felt a compelling need to confess, but because he had it really bad for his plainspoken young governess and her pointed censures. "Jane, I feel I can speak to you as freely as if I were writing my thoughts in a diary. Not three in three thousand raw school-girl governesses would bust my chops the way you do, and it really makes me hot. Please, punish me."

"While I do have a considerable background, gathered at the Lowell School, in the finer arts of discipline and physical punishment, I believe that what you need, Mr. Rochester, is not some Victorian dominatrix casting out your demons with each flick of her cat-o'-nine-tails, but a little twentieth-century psychoanalysis to help you get in touch with your inner child. I sense that there are difficult issues you are unwilling to confront, particularly when it comes to the women in your life, so let's talk about the batty babe in the belfry."

His eyes grew dark. A stormy countenance prevailed, with poor road conditions and a sixty percent chance of thunder showers by morning, and he spoke in low tones. "After a youth and manhood passed half in unutterable misery and half in dreary solitude, I have for the first time found what I can truly love—I have found *you*. You are my sympathy—my better self—my good angel—I am bound to you with a strong attachment."

"You're avoiding the issue."

"I think you good, gifted, lovely—"

"Do I sense a fear of confrontation?"

"Because I feel and know this, I am resolved to marry you. And just forget about the broad in the attic. She's just a poor plot device designed by some sexually frustrated quill-penned spinster to prevent me from getting my rocks off. So what do you say? Me, you, the French Riviera, long nights strolling along the Côte d'Azur, sipping champagne cocktails at the Negresco, you in a string bikini, me in a Speedo, as the sun sets?"

His proposition stunned her, for she had no inkling that the master of the house could ever love a plain Jane such as herself, particularly since she was far too self-conscious to wear a string bikini. Although she was drawn to glowering bad-boy types, she had a head full of negative thought patterns, clearly the residue of a deprived childhood, as she was informed by that article in *Psychology for Governesses*, which established a clear link between orphaned childhoods spent in drafty nineteenth-century institutions run by sadomasochistic headmasters and low self-esteem in later life. But she had managed to muster up enough confidence in her twenty-some-odd years on the planet to know that while she may have a poor body image, she was not a bigamist and told him so in no uncertain, overly protracted nineteenth-century terms.

"Mr. Rochester, I will not be yours. It would be bitter, wicked to marry you when I know, and you know, and you know I know, and I know you know I know that the babe in the belfry is your lawfully wedded wife."

He threw up his hands in tortured resignation. "So you

would condemn me to live wretched and to die accursed? Is there no remedy?"

This new vulnerable approach to their relationship's difficulties softened Jane's. She found herself smiling at him, remembering a little piece she'd just read in *Madwoman's Weekly* about revolutionary new advances in the treatment of bipolar illnesses, and she ventured, "Edward, sweetie, have you heard about these new wonder drugs they have been using in the treatment of the mentally ill? They are having marvelous success with few side effects, and I was wondering, perhaps your wife is suffering from a chemical imbalance. Maybe she can lead a perfectly healthy, normal life, free from extreme mood swings that manifest themselves in the form of violent, pyromaniacal outbursts. Why don't we send for a specialist who can prescribe an experimental course of the medication? Then, if it is effective, you can divorce her without guilt and we can put the past behind us."

Well, I was right about the wonder drugs. Mrs. Rochester is now a fully functional and independent woman happily running a gift shop in Kingston, Jamaica; in fact, she filed for a no-contest divorce, having met and become engaged to a rakish wayfarer with a hoop in his ear and a motherlode of plundered booty, which the tourists go mad for.

And Mr. Rochester? Reader, I married him, in a quiet ceremony in a small country church in the old village of Nice. We honeymooned there on the Côte d'Azur, swimming topless in the forgiving waters of the Mediterranean. Mr. Rochester seemed to have put his demons and his negative coping behaviors behind him and acquired a new lease on life as well as his own subscription to Governess Today—and I have become a featured columnist.

12

The Scarlet Letter

(Or, Beware the Fashion Police)

 throng of bearded men in sad-colored garments and gray steeple crowned hats intermixed with women, some wearing hoods and others bareheaded, was assembled in front of a wooden edifice, the door of which was heavily timbered with oak and studded with iron spikes. The grim rigidity that petrified the bearded physiognomies of these good people would have augured some awful business in hand—if only we could understand what the narrator was trying to betoken. Suffice to say it was a crowd of uptight Puritan super-Wasps just dying to cast the first stone at the dynamic woman of substance with the monogrammed frock standing before them on the parapet.

One particularly cranky woman, who probably hadn't gotten any since Plymouth Rock and was dressed in a horrible Spanish Inquisition–inspired hood and tunic ensemble with a waistline and collar—which did not do anything for her stout figure—stood up and addressed the dire assemblage.

"This woman has brought shame on us all and ought to die. She has given birth to a child out of wedlock and her attire is modeled much after her own fancy. And look at those fishnet DKNY stockings. Is there not law against it?"

Of course there was, because conspicuous consumption and instant gratification were capital offenses in Puritan Massachusetts circa 1642. No one forgave girls who just wanted to have fun, and alternative fashion statements were a class-one felony.

The sober Governor Bellingham arose, a dark feather in his hat, a border of embroidery in his cloak, and a black velvet tunic beneath. He addressed the fallen woman, whom he resented not only for the vileness of her sin but for her superior taste in casual day wear.

"Harken on to me, Hester Prynne, you have been found guilty of adultery and sentenced to live apart from us, and to bear the scarlet letter of your shame perpetually upon your breast. And so you have worn lo these two years the badge of shame, fashioned of fine red cloth, surrounded with an elaborate embroidery and fantastic flourishes of gold thread, artistically yet tastefully done, with so much fertility and gorgeous luxuriance of fancy and so splendorous that I could just spit. Either reveal the father of that child or I'm going to slap you silly. Dimmesdale, you are her pastor. Talk some sense into her."

The Reverend Mister Arthur Dimmesdale, a person of very striking aspect with large, brown melancholy eyes and a white lofty and impending brow (i.e., a hunk), expressing a vast power of self-restraint (i.e., a smoldering hunk), notwithstanding his high native gifts had an apprehensive air (i.e., a smoldering, well-hung, sensitive hunk). So far as his duties would permit, he trod in the shadowy bypaths (i.e., a smoldering, well-hung sensitive, misunderstood hunk) and thus kept himself simple and childlike, coming forth with a dewy purity of thought that many people said affected them like the speech of an angel (i.e., a smoldering, well-hung, sensitive, misunderstood, vulnerable hunk).

He was clad in a simple gray frock that accented his ethereal yet virile form with an understated elegance that matched Hester's own impeccable sense of style. One sensed that, although they were mix-and-match separates, together they would have made a fetching ensemble.

"Hester Prynne, if thou feelest it to be for thy soul's peace and that thy earthly punishment will be made more effectual to salvation, I charge thee to speak out the name of thy fellow sinner and fellow sufferer! Be not silent from any mistaken pity and tenderness for him, and do not show mercy because he knows how to accessorize as well as thou. For believe me, Hester, though he were to step down from a higher place, say, a pulpit, and stand there beside thee on the pedestal of shame, yet better were it so than to hide a guilty heart beneath a well-tailored and embroidered garment, say, a cassock. What can thy silence do for him except it tempt him to add hypocrisy to sin, which is as bad as mixing plaids and prints?"

"I will not speak," answered Hester, turning pale as death, "and though my fellow sufferer might step down from the greatest height, say, a pulpit, I'll still not relinquish my autonomous, self-sufficient lifestyle nor my trendsetting fashion sense in order to appease public opinion. Nor will I deem sinful that which is a natural expression of love between two consenting adults, although we should have used a condom and would have, had they been invented."

"Then return thee to thy cottage," said the governor, stomping his foot in a huff, "and we shall shun thee and speak not to thee, unless, of course, we need fashion tips or specialty beadwork done."

Late that night in her cottage, Hester received a visitor, a stranger to town who was practiced in the art of medicine. Roger Chillingworth had mastered the healing arts as well as a neoprimitive retro look featuring some stunning Pequot beadwork, having interned with the natives for nigh on two years and exploited their culture and art for his own shallow purposes, not properly compensating them for the use of their beadwork designs or medicinal formulas, ignoring all sense of morality or copyright law.

Hester gasped at the sight of him, not only because she recognized her long-lost and presumed dead husband, but because she noticed the Pequot detailing on his leather breechclout and was much impressed.

"I have greatly wronged thee, my husband," said Hester, clucking at the intricate styling at the base of the breech's clout. "I had no right to marry a man I did not love, placing my own need for security above the dictates of true passion. But truthfully, if you were going to be late, you should have called."

"It is true, I have wronged thee greater," said Chillingworth remorsefully. "Mine was the first wrong when I betrayed thy budding youth into a false and unnatural relation with my decay. And believe me, I couldn't find a pay phone anywhere. Be that as it may, as a man who has not thought and philosophized in vain, I seek no vengeance. Let me help to reunite you with the one who has captured your youthful ardor, and give your child a father. Tell me his name."

Hester bit her lip. "That thou shalt never know, for I have a deep-rooted fear of intimacy and commitment, stemming from my disastrous marriage to you. Let me be set apart, taking simple joy in my single parenthood and my successful cottage industry. Now go home and leave me be. I'm working on a new design for a simple evening sheath done in a stunning black chiffon silk with just a few poignant black pearls at the bodice and collar and I don't have time to sit around contemplating providence and the nature of good and evil in a repressed and puritanical society that doesn't appreciate haute couture."

Chillingworth assented to respect Hester's wishes and personal boundaries and departed, asking only that she might take a few moments some afternoon to show him how she managed that breathtaking appliqué on her red filigree gown.

Dimmesdale, however, could not find peace. He obsessed over his silent transgression and his hypocrisy, which clashed so revoltingly with his angelic image. He yearned to reunite with his soulmate, Hester Prynne, who brought harmony to the three-piece suit of his spirit, and longed to acknowledge his child, little Pearl. But he respected Hester's desire for space and her fear of commitment, and thus kept his silence.

Three years passed and finally Dimmesdale could bear it no more. He went to Hester and, threatening to inform the entire town of their clandestine romance, begged her to marry and make an honest man of him.

"Look, it won't be as bad as you think. I'm not going to encroach on your space. Hester, I respect your autonomy, your independent spirit, your incredible sense of color and texture, and your reluctance to engage in another relationship that may threaten the full life you have established for yourself and your child independent from the world of men and society and off-the-rack clothing. But you must understand, I wish to be your partner and ask only that you let me participate in the miracle of yourself and our daughter. We can go wherever you want—Paris, Milan, New York. I'll stay at home, I'll take care of little Pearl, and any other children you may choose to bless me with. I'll plan and prepare the meals, organize the household, and handle all of the details of your burgeoning cottage industry. Just so long as we are together, for I can't go on without you in my life as a full-fledged partner."

"Weeelll . . ." Hester began, "I want to make sure that you realize that when we forgot our God, when we violated our reverence, each for the other's soul, not by loving each other but by being silent, we were actually just working out of fear of public censure, which has no place in an intimate bond between two caring, trusting individuals. You are going to have to get over your fear of authority and need for social acceptance."

"I will, by my troth."

"And you are going to have to stop smoldering all the time. It's depressing."

"I can. Really, I won't smolder anymore."

"And all that fire and brimstone from the pulpit about sin and damnation is really a downer. What about a nurturing and loving God?"

"You got it. It's all New Testament from here on out."

"And you are going to have to do something about all that basic black. It's a new season for heaven's sake. Pastels are all the rage in Paris."

"It's powder blue and seafoam green for me from now on, my beloved."

"Well, all right, you seem sincere, but I'm a woman of means now and I can't afford to be making foolhardy decisions based on the impassioned vows of a smoldering and vulnerable, misunderstood, and admittedly well-hung hunk in a cassock. Let's live together first and see how things work out. Then we'll hammer out a prenup."

Reverend Mister Dimmesdale and Hester Prynne lived happily ever after. He became a contented house husband and Hester developed an internationally acclaimed collection called Hester Prynne's A-line, which catered to the needs of fashionable adulteresses worldwide.

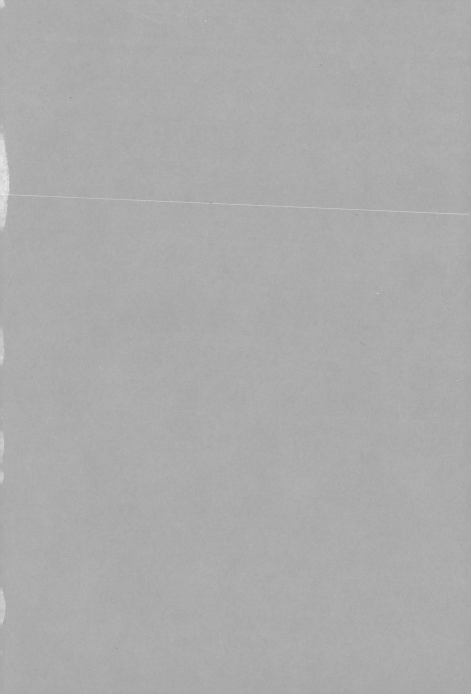